Jess Fogel

ARCO'S Little HOUSE

FOR ELIE AND THEO—JF

PENGUIN WORKSHOP
An imprint of Penguin Random House LLC
1745 Broadway, New York, New York 10019

First published simultaneously in paperback and hardcover in the United States of America by Penguin Workshop, an imprint of Penguin Random House LLC, 2025

Copyright © 2025 by Jess Fogel

Penguin Random House values and supports copyright. Copyright fuels creativity, encourages diverse voices, promotes free speech, and creates a vibrant culture. Thank you for buying an authorized edition of this book and for complying with copyright laws by not reproducing, scanning, or distributing any part of it in any form without permission. You are supporting writers and allowing Penguin Random House to continue to publish books for every reader. Please note that no part of this book may be used or reproduced in any manner for the purpose of training artificial intelligence technologies or systems.

PENGUIN is a registered trademark and PENGUIN WORKSHOP is a trademark of Penguin Books Ltd, and the W colophon is a registered trademark of Penguin Random House LLC.

Visit us online at penguinrandomhouse.com.

Library of Congress Cataloging-in-Publication Data is available.

Manufactured in China

ISBN 9780593523728 (hc)   10 9 8 7 6 5 4 3 2 1 TOPL

Design by Taylor Abatiell

The authorized representative in the EU for product safety and compliance is Penguin Random House Ireland, Morrison Chambers, 32 Nassau Street, Dublin D02 YH68, Ireland, https://eu-contact.penguin.ie

ARCO'S little HOUSE

BY JESS FOGEL

PENGUIN WORKSHOP

Arco loved his little house,
and he took good care of it.

In return, the little house took good care of Arco.

Then one day . . .

BANG!

BOOM!

DRILL!

"What a big, beautiful house!"

"Welcome, new neighbors!"

Wouldn't it be fun to have a big house?
Arco thought to himself.
Then I could run from room to room.

So Arco built himself a big house.

And he ran from room to room.

Wouldn't it be fun to have a house on wheels? Arco thought to himself. That way I could travel the world.

So Arco built himself a house on wheels.

And he started his travels.

He traveled far and wide.

And every new place Arco went, his house transformed a little more.

The more the house transformed,
the more admirers came.
The more admirers came,
the more the house transformed.

Everyone was excited, so Arco opened his door and invited them all in.

Winter came. Getting cozy in front of the woodstove was not so simple anymore.

Maybe this house is too complicated for me? thought Arco.

But the next morning, a bigger crowd arrived.
If everyone loves my house so much, then being cozy must not be important.

Finding things in the house became a real challenge.

Maybe this house is too big for me? thought Arco.

But the next morning an even BIGGER crowd arrived.

If everyone loves my house so much, then it must not be too big, thought Arco.

He felt a lump forming in his throat. This wasn't fun anymore.

"I want to go home," Arco whispered to the tree.

Arco stopped welcoming admirers, and he stopped taking care of his house.

And in return, his house could not take care of Arco anymore.

"It is not sad," Arco announced. "Because now I am going to build the perfect house. The perfect house for ME!"

So Arco built himself a little house.

And Arco loved it.
It was all he ever needed.